MONSTER MANOR

Von Skalpel's Experiment

by PAUL MARTIN and MANU BOISTEAU
Adapted by LISA PAPADEMETRIOU
Illustrated by MANU BOISTEAU

Hyperion Books for Children
New York

W9-AGZ-133

If you purchased this book without a cover, you should be aware that
this book is stolen property. It was reported as "unsold and destroyed"
to the publisher, and neither the author nor the publisher has received
any payment for this "stripped" book.

First published under the title *Maudit Manoir,*
Les Expériences de Von Skalpel
in France by Bayard Jeunesse.
© Bayard Editions Jeunesse, 2001
Monster Manor, Volo, and the Volo colophon
are trademarks of Disney Enterprises, Inc.

All rights reserved. No part of this book may be reproduced or transmitted
in any form or by any means, electronic or mechanical, including
photocopying, recording, or by any information storage and retrieval system,
without written permission from the publisher. For information address
Volo Books, 114 Fifth Avenue, New York, New York 10011-5690.

Printed in the United States of America
First U.S. edition, 2003
1 3 5 7 9 10 8 6 4 2
This book is set in 13-point Excelsior.

ISBN 0-7868-1719-4

Visit www.volobooks.com

Make way for the monsters from
MONSTER MANOR

Contents

*I*f you're ever in Transylvaniaville, be sure to stop by Mon Staire Manor. Everyone calls it *Monster* Manor... that's because a bunch of monsters live there.

The Haunted Hills

Nerdburg

Transylvaniaville

Malibu Nightclub

MƎLIBU

A Scary-looking Tree

The Slippen Falls

There are lots of fun things to do at the Manor. You can stroll through the cemetery, watch the swamp glow under the moonlight, or make a few new friends!

The FEMUR Family

EYE-GORE & STEVE

This sweet little family may look scary, but the truth is that they have no guts at all.

They want to be skate punks, but they're really just zombies with bad attitudes.

BEATRICE Mon Staire

She's haunted by a horrible secret... and a hairdo that's even worse.

Wolf Man STU

When the moon is full, he becomes human. Well, *somewhat* human...

COUNT SNOBULA

He isn't rich, but he *is* totally stuck up. Thank goodness he sleeps all day.

Step through the gate—
let's see who's home!

The SWAMP HORROR

SALLY the Specter

Professor VON SKALPEL

It ain't easy being a big green ball of toxic slime!

Beatrice's mother is smart, sassy—and a ghost!

The most brilliant mad scientist in town. He's a real cutup.

FRANKIE

Created by Von Skalpel,
Frankie is one of a kind.
Thank goodness.

Take a look inside the Manor.
It might be old, but the monsters
think of it as "home, sweet home."

Von Skalpel's
Room

The Very
Secret

Von Ska
Labora

The
Femur Crypt

Eye-Gore
and
Steve's Pit

The Radioactive Swamp

If you dare come inside, beware!
The professor might think you
have a screw loose!

CHAPTER ONE
The End?

Professor Von Skalpel looked closely at the bubbling test tubes. His dark glasses made watching the experiment difficult, but the professor never took them off. Some people said it was because he worked with electricity and didn't want to risk being blinded by flashes of light. Some said it was because his experiments were so ghastly that he didn't want to see them. But only Von Skalpel knew the truth—he thought the glasses made him look cool.

1

"In a moment, my experiment vill be complete," Professor Von Skalpel muttered. The professor had an accent, but no one was sure where he was from. "Zen I can—yee-haa-haa-yikes!"

Actually, "yee-haa-haa-yikes" wasn't part of the professor's plan. He shouted it because he was startled by a loud knock at the door. A loud, wet, slimy-sounding knock.

The door creaked open. There stood a creature. The thing was enormous—almost as wide as it was tall—and made of green slime.

"Horror!" the professor shouted. He ran to the back of the laboratory. The sticky creature dribbled. *Splat!* And then the creature took a heavy, wet step into the lab.

What did the creature want from Von Skalpel?

Could this be *THE END*?

Get real—of course not. It's only chapter one.

Horror was this monster's name, and he happened to be the professor's pal. Why? Well...

When Professor Herman Von Skalpel had decided to move into Mon Staire Manor, everyone told him he was crazy. Of course, people often told the professor that he was crazy, so he really didn't think much of it. Professor Von Skalpel had heard all of the rumors before. He knew that the people in Transylvaniaville called Mon Staire Manor "Monster Manor." People warned him about the horrifying, nightmarish creatures that lived there. He knew that the villagers said the house was haunted.

And that was exactly why he wanted to live there.

The professor needed a place to do his experiments. Von Skalpel wanted to create chocolate–watermelon–peanut butter–anchovy–flavored chewing gum. There was only one problem—no one ever wanted to test a piece.

The professor needed someone to sample his gum for him, so he dug up some body parts from the local cemetery and brought them to life with the power of static electricity. But ever since he had created his loyal assistant, Frankie, the professor had become obsessed with creating new creatures. In fact, some people thought that he would never go back to his chewing-gum research at all. (Those people were relieved.) But everyone agreed that there was no better place for someone who creates monsters than a place like Monster Manor.

And that's why the professor wasn't afraid of the enormous, slimy, green monster in the doorway. In fact, they were neighbors. The Swamp Horror lived in the radioactive swamp nearby.

The Swamp Horror coughed.

"Let me guess," the professor said as he reached into a cabinet at the rear of his laboratory. "You have got anozer cold."

Horror nodded miserably. The fact was, the

marsh where he lived was quite damp, and it often gave him the sniffles. "Sorry to bother you, Professor," the Swamp Horror said. "It's just that I can't stop sneez—ah—ah—"

"Do not dare sneeze in here!" the professor cried. "I vas cleaning slime off zee valls for two montz zee last time." He handed the Swamp Horror a tissue.

Horror blew his nose. The sound was like an enormous set of bagpipes getting stepped on by an elephant.

"Let us see..." the professor said as he peered into his cabinet. "Verevolf Hairball Reducer...Specter Deflector...Ah—here vee are!" He handed Horror a can of something that looked like tar. "Venemox."

Horror put his finger in the goo and tasted it. "Not bad," he admitted.

"Do not sound so surprised," the professor said. "It is snake egg–butterscotch flavor."

Horror frowned. "What's it made of?" he asked.

"Oh, zis and zat..." the professor said. Seeing Horror's frown, he admitted, "It is mostly drain cleaner."

Horror shrugged. "Okay," he said, and took a gulp of the Venemox.

"Now, if you vill excuse me," Von Skalpel said, "I have some very important vork to do."

"Thanks a lot, Doc," Horror said happily. "I'm feeling better already!"

Just as the professor went to close his supply cabinet, there was a horrible thudding noise behind him. Few people in the world were clumsy enough to make that much noise. Von Skalpel didn't need to turn around to know who was there.

8

"Hello, Frankie," he said. "You are late."

"Sorry, Professor!" Frankie said sheepishly. "I overslept."

"Vere you up late vatching *Zee Young and zee Undead* again?"

Frankie shuffled his feet and nodded.

"Vell, you had better vake up," the professor said. "Because vee are starting a brand-new experiment today."

Frankie grinned. He was missing some

teeth and had a bunch of scars. The professor sighed. Frankie was very sweet, but horribly ugly and very clumsy. Ever since Von Skalpel had brought him to life using the electric charge he got from socks that were fresh from the dryer, the professor wanted to make a creature that was more...perfect. Someone handsome, and witty. Someone worthy to be the assistant of a brilliant mad scientist.

But the professor had a problem. A creature made by sewing together body parts would always have scars. So—how could Professor Von Skalpel create someone with a smooth complexion? The question had plagued Von Skalpel for months.

Until now...

CHAPTER TWO
Monster Glue

"Frankie, today vee are going to test my latest *brilliant* invention."

"What is it?" Frankie asked eagerly.

The professor held out a beaker. "Behold!" he cried. "I give you...Monster Glue!"

Frankie stared at the glue blankly. "What does it do?" he asked.

"Do I have to explain everysing?" the professor demanded.

"Huh?" Frankie thought for a moment. "Yes."

"Good point," Von Skalpel replied. "Viz Monster Glue, I can create new creatures vizout sewing and ugly scars. A dab of Monster Glue is enough to attach an arm, or an ear, or even a belly button!"

At that moment, the professor was hit on the head with something hard.

"Thorry!" shouted a voice at Professor Von Skalpel's feet.

The minute the stars cleared the professor's eyes, he looked down to see little Bonehead Femur. Actually, what he saw was only Bonehead's skull. "You seem to have lost your head," the professor observed.

"You might thay that," Bonehead admitted. The little skull had a lisp. "Or you might thay I've *kept* my head and losht the resht of me."

"Vhere is your body?" the professor asked.

"In the living room," Bonehead said. "I wath watching TV with Wolf Man Thtu. He wanted to change the channel. When I tried to thtop him, he got angry. Then he plucked off my head and tothed it into the hall!"

"Really," the professor grumbled as he picked up the skull and tucked it under his arm. "Some of zeez monsters have no manners at all!" Grabbing his tube of glue, he headed for the door.

"Um, Profethor?" Bonehead asked in a muffled voice. "Could you turn me around tho that my fathe ithn't in your armpit?"

The Manor's living room was filled with life-size portraits of the Mon Staire family. Their eyes glared down at visitors. At the far end of the room was a large, battered television set. Professor Von Skalpel had given it as a gift to the house when he moved in. It had made him instantly popular.

"Volf Man Schtu!" the professor shouted, holding Bonehead's skull aloft. "Vhat do you have to say about zis?" Von Skalpel walked into the living room where the wolf man was watching TV.

Wolf Man Stu eyed the round, white skull

coolly. "Anyone for volleyball?" he asked.

"Zis is not a joke!" the professor cried. "You cannot go around attacking skeletons!"

"I was just defending myself!" the were-wolf insisted. "That kid tried to grab the remote control right out of my hand!"

"That'th a lie!" Bonehead yelled.

"What's going on here?" demanded a female voice behind them.

The professor cringed. He knew that voice. It belonged to Beatrice Mon Staire, the landlady.

Get the name right!

The professor turned and gave her a low bow. "My dear Miss Monster—"

"It's Mon *Staire*," she correc-ted him through clenched teeth.

"Ah—yes—vhatever," the pro-fessor said quickly. "I vas just going to say zat I have zis problem under control."

"All I know is that you're making enough noise to raise the dead," Beatrice said dryly. "And you know how cranky Mother gets when she hasn't had enough sleep." (Beatrice's mother is a ghost—but don't tell *her* that.)

"Ah, yes, vell—vee vill try to keep zee noise to a level zat only disturbs zee living." The professor chuckled, then cleared his throat and changed the subject. "Bonehead, I have got just zee sing for you," he said. "Schtu— help me to gather up zee rest of Bonehead's body." The professor picked up a leg lying nearby and looked at it carefully. "Vere you *gnawing* on zis?" he asked the wolf man.

"Of course not!" Stu said quickly. He grabbed the bone and put it back in place with the rest of the skeleton.

Professor Von Skalpel squirted a bit of his

latest invention at the base of Bonehead's skull. Then he pressed the skull against the rest of the body and counted to ten. "Zere—" the professor said. "It is dry. You are good as new, Bonehead."

Bonehead turned his skull right and left, testing it. "Crypt-acular, Profethor!" he cried.

"Now I can watch my favorite show—*Tomb of Terror!*"

"Forget it, *Block*head," Stu grumbled. "*Howl at the Moon* is coming on."

"Give me that!" Bonehead said, grabbing at the remote in the werewolf's hand.

Beatrice gave the professor a sideways look. Shaking his head, Von Skalpel unplugged the TV.

"Hey!" Wolf Man Stu and Bonehead said. The professor took the TV cord and put it in the pocket of his lab coat.

"I have a very important experiment to do zat reqvires a great deal of electricity," the professor said. "You vill have to find anozer vay to amuse yourselves for a vhile."

Wolf Man Stu and Bonehead left, grumbling.

The professor walked Beatrice to the stairs that led to her apartment. "Professor, you handled that very well," Beatrice said. "These monsters can get out of control if you don't show them who's boss." She pounded her fist against the banister with such force that the professor winced.

When Von Skalpel walked into the lab, he saw that Frankie had prepared everything for the experiment. All the professor had to do was to put together the creature and pull a few static-cling–charged socks from the dryer.

Then, if all went well, there would be a hip new monster on the block.

CHAPTER THREE
The New Monster on the Block

When the clock struck midnight, Monster Manor came alive... well, as alive as a manor filled with vampires, skeletons, and zombies can be. Wolf Man Stu and Bonehead joined Radius, Tibia, and Kneecap Femur in the living room. Behind them were Eye-Gore and Steve, the grouchy teenage zombies. Count Snobula rose from his crypt behind the boiler while Beatrice Mon Staire fed her beloved dead and man-eating plants in the green-house. Finally, Sally Mon Staire—Beatrice's mother and the only genuine ghost in the Manor—appeared.

"Well, bless my dear departed soul," Sally said as she floated into the living room, "I do believe the entire Manor is here to watch TV."

"The professor stole the TV cord," Wolf

I could tell you a few good ghost stories....

PFFF

Man Stu growled. He threw back his head and let out a deafening howl.

"This stinks," Eye-Gore said in a raspy monotone. "I'm bored."

"Perhaps we should play a game?" Count Snobula suggested. "Does anyone know how to play bridge?"

"I do," Sally said quickly. Everyone looked at the floor. None of the monsters liked playing cards with Sally because she could turn invisible and look at everyone else's cards. Although no one had actually *seen* Sally cheat, she did insist on playing while invisible—she said it helped her think. She always won.

Suddenly, the lights went out.

"Really, Beatrice, this is getting absurd," Count Snobula said in the darkness. "The lights go out whenever the professor runs that dryer of his. How much laundry can one man have? I think it's high time that you spoke to him."

Beatrice sighed. "Why don't *you* speak to him, Snobula?"

The lights came back on.

"Well, I *would* speak to him," the Count said, "but it's *your* house."

Just then, the professor walked into the room, his fist raised in triumph. Frankie was right behind him. "My friends," Von Skalpel said happily, "I apologize for zee temporary blackout. I have brought you—"

"The TV cord?" Bonehead asked eagerly as he slid out from beneath the table. He had just finished tying Wolf Man Stu's tail to his chair with an old shoelace.

"No," the professor said patiently. "My latest creation—Frankie, bring him in!"

There was a loud thud and the sound of a giant footstep. The room shook as an enormous monster walked into the room. He looked like a giant bowl of lime Jell-O with eyeballs and body parts floating in it.

"Wow!" Kneecap said. She was Bonehead's little sister, and easily impressed.

But even Bonehead thought the monster was cool. In fact, all of the monsters except Wolf Man Stu gathered around the creation to get a better look. Stu was, of course, still tied to his chair.

"He hath five legth!" Bonehead cried.

"And nine eyes," Eye-Gore said. "That's radical!"

"Actually, zere are eleven," the professor corrected. "Two on zee back."

The monster took a step to the right with one foot, and a step to the left with another. He swayed for a moment, unable to move in either direction, until a third foot stepped forward. Everyone else stepped away.

"What does he . . . do?" Count Snobula asked.

"Do?" Professor Von Skalpel seemed surprised by the question. "Vell, he does not really *do* anysing. Zis is just a sample of my latest, greatest invention—Monster Glue!"

He held out his arms in a *ta-da!* gesture. The monsters looked at one another. Nobody spoke.

"Do you not see?" the professor asked. "From now on, I can make all sorts of monsters, faster zan ever before." He pointed to Frankie, who was watching with a confused expression. "And none of zem vill have scars, because zere is no stitching reqvired. Zat is right, ladies and gentlemen, dead and alive! Zis is a new era. And zee glue dries almost instantly—right, Bonehead?"

"Uh...yeah," Bonehead said.

Tibia Femur, Bonehead's mother, frowned. "What's this all about?"

Bonehead kicked at the carpet. "My head fell off, and the profethor glued it back on for me."

I could uthe thome good glue.

"My goodness!" Tibia put her hand over the place where her heart would have been. "Professor, this is wonderful!" There was a general buzz as the monsters admired the professor's handiwork. Steve stepped closer to the new creature to examine how the parts were

assembled. Even Count Snobula admitted that the professor's work was, in this case, "Brilliant."

The professor was grinning, when he suddenly felt a thump on his back. He turned to see Frankie, who had tapped him on the back as gently as he could.

"Excuse me, Professor, but the creature—" Frankie said.

"Is amazing, is he not?" the professor interrupted.

Frankie nodded. "Yes, but he's—"

"He is zee new cutting edge in creature creation," the professor went on. "I vonder if he vould enjoy chewving gum? It seems to me—"

"Professor, the creature is falling apart!" Frankie cried.

"Vhat?" Professor Von Skalpel turned and saw that his creature was looking very ill.

Something horrible was happening. There was a gurgling sound as the creature's eyeballs began to pop off. One of them rolled across Beatrice Mon Staire's foot, and she let out a little scream. Then one of the creature's arms fell off.

"Frankie, help me to take him back to zee laboratory before he totally loses it!" the professor cried.

Frankie hurried toward the creature to help, but it was too late. Organs and body parts were falling fast. It was like watching autumn leaves drop from a tree, only much, much messier.

Bonehead let out a shriek and went running after a hand that was letting its fingers do the walking. "I'll get it!" he cried...just as his head fell off and went rolling across the floor.

"Ahhhhhh!" Bonehead cried as his skull rolled under the dinner table. "I'm broken again!" Bonehead's headless body ran about the room madly until it ran into a wall and fell to the floor in a heap.

Tibia reached under the table and grabbed Bonehead's skull. "Oh, my poor baby!" she cried. "Mommy will kiss it and make it better." She gave the base of Bonehead's skull a quick peck.

"I don't feel any better," Bonehead told her.

"I'll put you in a cast and you'll be fine in the morning," Tibia promised quickly. "Clearly, the professor's glue is garbage."

"Now, vait!" The professor rubbed his head. He did that when he was thinking hard. "Maybe I just did not use enough glue. Perhaps I can—"

"No, Tibia is right," said an angry voice from the back of the room. "The professor is a quack!"

CHAPTER FOUR
Quack, Quack, Quack!

The Swamp Horror stood in the doorway looking even grosser than usual.

"What's the matter with you?" Sally asked. "You look like poop."

It was true. His usual bright green color was now a dingy brown.

"This morning the professor gave me one of his mixtures—a cold remedy called Venemox. Now look at me!" the Swamp Horror said with a cough. "And my cold has gotten worse, too."

Everyone turned to stare at the professor. Eye-Gore's right eye bounced out of its socket.

"I do not know vhat happened!" the professor said. "Zee Venemox vorks perfectly...." Von Skalpel stroked his chin thoughtfully. "Maybe it vas affected by zee svamp's radioactivity. Horror, I can give you a skin cream zat vill clear you right up—"

"No thanks," the Swamp Horror said quickly. "The last time I used your cream I broke out in pimples. From now on, I think I'll make my own cold remedies."

"Why do we let the professor hang out with us, anyway?" Eye-Gore demanded. "He unplugs the TV, he turns off the lights, and he takes all of the good body parts out of the cemetery!"

"He isn't even a monster," Count Snobula agreed.

Professor Von Skalpel glanced nervously at the angry faces around him. "Vell, many of my closest friends are monsters," he pointed out, "and my hobby is *making* monsters...." At that moment, a foot hopped between the professor's legs. Suddenly remembering his failed experiment, the professor turned to look around the room. Body parts were everywhere! They were bouncing on the furniture, swinging from the chandelier, and generally going crazy. An elbow scuttled toward the window in a desperate attempt to be free.

"Do not let zem get avay!" the professor shouted.

"Especially the bones," Radius Femur agreed. "You never know when we might need them!"

A set of teeth chattered after Beatrice, who let out a scream. At the door was a large intestine that had wound itself across the exit like a gross, slimy spiderweb.

A hairy hand attached itself to Count Snobula's ankle. The snobby vampire nearly fainted. "Oh, my," he said woozily.

Sally disappeared. Wolf Man Stu barked twice and began chasing something madly. It took him ten minutes to realize he was chasing his own tail—and the chair it was tied to. The only ones who seemed to be having fun were Kneecap and Bonehead, who ran after a bunch of rolling eyes as though they were rubber balls.

With all the confusion, the professor took

the opportunity to duck behind the drapes.

"Where are you, Von Skalpel?" the Swamp Horror shouted. Scooping up a skinny leg, he added, "You think you're a brilliant scientist, eh? I'll show you what it feels like to put your foot in your mouth!"

Swamp Horror looked around, but couldn't find the professor anywhere. Beatrice and the Femurs leapt over the large intestine, and Count Snobula followed them. The two zombies had climbed out the window, and Wolf Man Stu had finally untied himself from the chair and escaped. Horror took a final glance around the room. The professor seemed to have disappeared, too.

Professor Von Skalpel counted to one hundred before coming out from his hiding place. When he finally looked out from behind the curtain, there was only one monster left in the room.

Frankie was tidying up as well as he could.

"Is everyvun gone?" the professor whispered.

"Yeah," Frankie said, sweeping a nose and two ears into a pile of body parts. "And I think these little guys are getting tired."

The professor stared at the pile and shook his head sadly. "I sink I vill go to bed, Frankie," he said.

Frankie nodded and kept sweeping. "See you in the morning, Professor!" he sang.

Von Skalpel nodded and shuffled to his room to get ready for bed. As he turned out the light, he hoped that things weren't as bad as they seemed. "Maybe all I need is a good night of rest," the professor told himself. "I am sure sings vill look brighter in zee morning."

CHAPTER FIVE
Things Do Not Look Brighter

The professor woke up the next morning feeling as though he had the weight of the world on his shoulders. When he slowly opened his eyes he saw why—the large intestine that had blocked the doorway the night before was now wrapped around the professor like a boa constrictor.

"Frankie!" the professor said with a gasp. "Fra-a-a-a-aaaaaggggnnnccccckkk!" The intestine was really squeezing now.

Frankie wasn't very smart and he certainly wasn't very good-looking—but his hearing was excellent. He rushed through the Manor as quickly as he could.

"Professor!" he cried as he burst into the room, knocking the door off its hinges. "What's wrong?"

"Gaaacckk!" Von Skalpel cried. The intestine had tightened its hold on the professor, and he could hardly breathe or speak. "Gaaacckk!"

Frankie scratched his head. "What?"

"Geeeg giiiig gaaaccckk!" the professor cried, which roughly translated into "Get zis sing off me!" Not that Frankie knew that.

"I'm sorry, Professor," Frankie said. "I don't understand what you're saying." He stared at the intestine. "I hope you don't mind

41

if I take this off," he said as he pulled it off and sent the professor spinning off his bed and onto the floor.

The professor wheezed and coughed in an effort to catch his breath. "Sank you, Frankie!" he said.

"What did you want?" Frankie asked. "Breakfast?"

Von Skalpel stared at Frankie a moment, then decided not to bother explaining to him. "Sure," the professor said. "Breakfast vould be good."

But when Frankie pointed to the table, the professor lost his appetite. First, there was an eyeball floating in his cereal. And when he reached for a piece of bread to make toast, he saw that there was a hand sticking out of the toaster. "Zis is going to be vun of zose days,"

Von Skalpel muttered as he poured his cereal—eyeball and all—into the garbage.

The professor realized that he had to do something about the body parts he had unleashed on the Manor. He grabbed a sack for the organs, then walked into the hall and nearly tripped over a casket.

"Do you *mind*?" Radius asked. "Some of us would like to get a little shut-eye."

Von Skalpel wanted to point out that skeletons don't have *eyes*, but there was an even bigger question on his mind. "Vhat are you doing here?" he asked. "And vhy are you using inflatable coffins?"

"These are the coffins we use for *camping*," Tibia snapped. "We're staying here until we can go back to our crypt. This is what you've driven us to, Von Skalpel!" Her little dog, Funnybone, gave a low growl, and the professor edged away.

"Me?" the professor asked. "But I have not done any experiments in zee cemetery."

"Oh, really?" Radius asked, folding his arms across his rib cage. "Then where are our children? And where did the mons—ouch!"

Radius rubbed his skull where he had just been kicked. A scrawny green leg hopped away. Funnybone ran after it, yapping.

"Come back, Funnybone!" Tibia wailed.

Von Skalpel winced. The body parts were out of control, and it was all his fault. He knew that he had to help in any way he could.

"I vill catch your dog," Von Skalpel said. "And I do not know vere your children are, but I promise to find zem. I know zis manor like zee back of my hand." The professor held his hand before his face to demonstrate. Frowning, he peered at his index finger. "Vhere did zat little mole come from?"

Tibia clutched her head. "I'll never see my children again!" she wailed.

"I vill have zem back before you know it," Von Skalpel promised. "And your little dog, too!" he added, hurrying after Funnybone. It wasn't hard—all he had to do was follow the sound of the dog's yapping. Von Skalpel wound his way up a spiral staircase and through the attic, and finally came to a dead end. Or was it?

Von Skalpel could hear Funnybone's hoarse little yips on the other side of the wall. This had to be a secret passageway. The professor felt along the wall for a few moments, but couldn't find a lever anywhere. Frustrated, he pounded the wall a few times with his fist.

With a great groan, the wall moved aside.

"Gadzooks!" the professor cried as he stepped into the passageway. "I have done it." The hall was dark and damp, and the corridor echoed with each of the professor's footsteps. The hairs at the back of the professor's head prickled, and he realized that he wasn't alone. "Oooh—ya-ha-yikes!" Von Skalpel shouted as he stepped on something squishy. When he drew his foot away, the thing—which looked like a giant slug—scurried over to a corner to join its friends. Once the professor's eyes adjusted to the dim light, he realized what the things in the corner were: body parts from his creature.

"Aha!" the professor cried, holding up his sack. "I have got you now!" The organs and limbs made a dash for it, but the professor managed to grab a couple of kidneys, a stomach, a liver, two legs, and a nose before they escaped. There was only one thing left in the corner. It was a hairy thing that the professor guessed was the creature's wig. It looked like a bad toupee that had come to life.

"You cannot escape," Von Skalpel said as he lunged at the toupee. But the hair was too quick—it rolled away like a small, furry Hula-Hoop.

"Come back here!" the professor cried as he ran down the hall after it. But the toupee was too fast. When the wig reached the end of the hall, it flattened itself out and wriggled under the door.

"Vhy did I not make a *bald* monster?" Von Skalpel asked with a groan. At least this time he knew what to do to get out of the secret passageway. Quickly, he banged his fist against the secret door.

"Aaagh!" cried a voice.

The professor looked down. He was standing on a mass of hair. "Gadzooks!" the professor cried. "I have created a talking toupee!"

But before he could begin to think of the moneymaking possibilities of such an invention, the voice snarled, "Get off my tail, Von Skalpel!"

"Volf Man Schtu!" the professor cried. The

werewolf stood there holding the television, fangs bared. "Vhat are you doing viz zee TV?"

"Taking it back to my kennel," Wolf Man Stu replied.

"Put it down right now," Von Skalpel said. "I bought zat for zee house!"

"You're not the boss of me!" Wolf Man Stu growled, then stomped his foot. "Everyone thinks they can order me around—don't you people understand that I'm a dangerous wild beast of the night and deserve a little *respect*? Even that kid skeleton thinks he can tell me what to watch. I'm sick of it! You hear? Sick of it!" With that, the werewolf threw back his head and let out a deafening howl.

The professor covered his ears. "Qvit howling—you vill vake zee vampire," he said. "Fine. Take zee TV if you vant it so badly."

"I *can't*," Wolf Man Stu said.

"I knew you vould change your mind," the professor said.

"I haven't," Wolf Man Stu said. "You're standing on my tail."

"Oh." Von Skalpel lifted his foot. "Sorry."

The werewolf growled and skulked away with the television.

Sighing, the professor looked around empty living room. The toupee was nowhere to be found, Funnybone had completely disappeared, and all of the monsters were mad at him.

"At least I should look on zee bright side," Professor Von Skalpel said to himself. "Vhen sings are zis bad, zey cannot possibly get any vorse."

CHAPTER SIX
Things Can Possibly Get Worse

A long, dark shadow fell across the room. The size of it sent a chill down the professor's spine. "Maybe it is just a small monster casting a large shadow," he told himself hopefully as he turned to see.

The professor gulped. The thing standing in the doorway was *not* a small monster. In fact, it was enormous—taller than any monster Von Skalpel had ever seen, which is saying something. It had a crooked body draped in a long green coat. Its four hairy hands hung out of the sleeves at unequal lengths.

"Vha-vha-vhat do you vant?" the professor stammered.

"Gurglaah!" The creature had an alarming high-pitched voice. "Gurglaah!" It took a lurching step forward—and lost its head.

"Yikes!" The professor jumped behind the sofa and crouched there, quaking.

"You cannot ethcape!" the creature cried.

"Ethcape?" the professor repeated. In all his years, Von Skalpel had only met one monster with a lisp. Carefully, the professor peeked over the side of the couch. The creature stood still, swaying awkwardly. "Hmm." Von Skalpel had an idea. Quickly, he ripped off the creature's coat. "Bonehead Femur!" he yelled. Bonehead's sister was standing on his

shoulders. "Kneecap! You hooligans! Vait until your parents hear zat you have been making monsters out of body parts! Vhere did you come up viz such an idea?"

"Run!" Kneecap cried. "Run!"

The skeletons turned and dashed away, moving quickly atop the extra-large legs of their costume. The professor hurried after them as they slipped out the back door. "Zose two cannot get avay," he said under his breath. "Zey vill run into zee radioactive svamp. Ha-ha!" The professor laughed as he thought of the lecture he would give the skeletons when he caught up to them. If there was one thing the professor truly enjoyed, it was giving a long, boring lecture.

Splash! The professor arrived at the swamp just in time to see the two young Femurs paddling for the far shore. Their disguise broke apart and floated away from them.

"Hooligans!" Professor Von Skalpel cried, shaking his fist. "You cannot run avay from me forev—ah!"

The professor bent to examine the body parts that had floated toward him, and noticed that they *all* seemed larger than he remembered. And when he tried to shove them into his bag, he realized that they had definitely gotten stronger. What was going on? Had they been exercising?

Suddenly, the professor remembered that Radius Femur had accused him of doing experiments in the cemetery. Was something strange going on in the graveyard? Von Skalpel was determined to find out.

The professor gave the air a big sniff, and was met with a familiar odor. "Venemox!" the professor cried, following his nose toward the cemetery.

The smell was particularly strong behind the Femur Family tomb. There, the professor found the can he had given the Swamp Horror.

Pecking at it was a gross three-eyed chick-adee.

"I can't believe it," the professor whispered. "Zee Svamp Horror is a litterbug!"

Nearby was a pile of overgrown body parts. "Zose little skeletons have been pouring the Venemox on my creature pieces—zen zey took the best vuns and made zeir own monster!" The professor frowned. "Vhy did I not sink of zat?"

The professor picked up the almost empty can and hurried away. He'd just had an idea. And a brilliant idea like this one might just be enough to make the other monsters forget about all of the trouble he'd caused. . . .

We must hurry! The sun is coming up.

CHAPTER SEVEN
Monster Conga!

Meanwhile, back at the Manor, the other monsters were having a meeting in the living room.

"Now he's really gone too far," Count Snobula proclaimed. "I tell you, he's gone mad!"

"If the professor thinks he can just take our television set," Eye-Gore growled, "he's about to think different." He pounded his fist into his palm so hard his eyeballs jiggled.

"Where is Von Skalpel now?" Tibia asked. She'd just finished tucking Bonehead and Kneecap into their inflatable coffins. "And poor Funnybone—I haven't seen him all day."

"I want to watch *Tales from the Grave*," Steve complained. "It's my favorite show!"

The monsters broke into a noisy chorus of complaints. All except for Wolf Man Stu, who was strangely silent. He did not want to tell the others that he was the one who had taken the television set. Let them pick on one another for a change.

"Quiet, everyone!" Beatrice Mon Staire commanded. The room fell instantly silent. "This bickering isn't getting us anywhere. Clearly, the professor has taken the television set, and the only way we'll get it back is to get it ourselves."

Sally folded her arms across her chest. "Oh, yeah? Well, how do you suggest we do that—ransack his laboratory?"

"Excellent!" Count Snobula raised his glass of blood toward Sally. "My good woman, I salute you and your brilliant idea!"

"I'm with Sally and the vampire," Steve said.

"Yeah!" Eye-Gore agreed.

"Now, wait just a minute," Radius protested. "I have to point out that the TV belonged to the professor in the first place...."

Beatrice raised an eyebrow and frowned at the skeleton. "Mr. Femur, weren't those your family's inflatable coffins I saw in *my* hallway this evening?"

The skeleton seemed rattled. "And now that I've pointed that out, I feel that we can go right ahead," Radius finished.

"The sooner the better," the Swamp Horror—who was looking much better after a good day's soak in the steaming swamp—said. "Who knows what he's cooking up in there?"

"Everyone, follow me!" Sally cried. "To the lab!" Then she swung her hips and sang, "Let's all go and ran-SACK!"

Beatrice fell in behind her mother, forming a conga line. "Let's all go and ran-SACK!"

Everyone joined in. "Let's all go and ran-SACK! Von Skalpel is a big QUACK! We'll get

the TV right BACK!" They pranced around the living room, singing at the top of their lungs.

The monsters were happy. The monsters were triumphant. The monsters were—

"*Grr*—get off my tail or I'll bite you!"

Well, let's face it, the monsters were terrible dancers.

"I didn't mean to step on you!" the Swamp Horror protested. "Try moving a little faster?"

"*Grr*—I get no respect around here!" Wolf Man Stu cried. "It's time I taught you a lesson!"

"Really, Stu, you're acting quite *beastly*," Count Snobula said with a sniff. "Of course, I suppose that's the best we can expect from someone like you."

"Why, you—" The werewolf lunged at the vampire.

"My cape!" Count Snobula cried. "Let me go, this cape is pure silk!"

"It tastes like polyester," Wolf Man Stu replied, the cape still in his mouth.

"Don't talk with your mouth full," the vampire scolded him.

Wolf Man Stu was about to give the snobby vampire a lesson in manners when he felt

himself lifted into the air. "What's going on?" he cried.

Looking around, Wolf Man Stu realized that all of the other monsters had backed into a corner, and were looking with frightened faces at whatever was behind him. The werewolf gulped. He had a feeling that, whatever the thing was...it wasn't going to give him any respect.

CHAPTER EIGHT
Everybody Loves Momo

Wolf Man Stu looked behind him and saw a horrifying sight: a monster had him by the tail. But it wasn't just any monster—it was *huge*.

The creature's jaws opened.

"He's going to bite me!" Wolf Man Stu shrieked. "Somebody help me!"

But nobody wanted to take on a creature *that* size. The other monsters backed away.

The thing pointed at Wolf Man Stu.

"Be . . . nice," the creature said.

The werewolf fainted.

Everyone watched as the creature set Stu down gently. Count Snobula stood up and straightened his tie. "Thank you, my good man," he said to the horrifying thing. "Honestly, that was the most disgraceful show of poor manners I've ever seen from a werewolf."

"This creature looks familiar," the Swamp Horror said slowly as he stared at the blue blob. It was wearing a little hat that read, "Momo."

"Hee-hee!" A giggle floated up from behind the creature's ankle.

"The creature's foot is laughing at us!" Radius cried.

"Now, see here," Count Snobula told the creature's ankle sternly. "You can't come here and laugh at us!"

"Hee-hee!" Professor Von Skalpel stepped out from behind the creature's leg. "It is too late, Snobula," he said. "People have been laughing at you for zee last seven hundred years!"

"Is this creature yours, Von Skalpel?" Beatrice demanded.

"Vhy, yes," the professor said patting his creation on the knee. "Everyvun, I'd like you to meet Momo."

"Is he—safe?" the Swamp Horror asked.

"He is as gentle as a lamp," the professor replied.

"You mean, 'as gentle as a lamb,'" Sally corrected.

"Vhich is more gentle, a lamb or a lamp?" the

professor demanded. "He is as gentle as a lamp, I tell you. And as vell built—sanks to my new and improved Monster Glue!"

"He certainly is . . . large," Beatrice said.

"Yes," the professor agreed, "and look at vhat he can do." He handed Momo a feather duster, and the creature instantly began to clean the chandelier.

"Vee vill never need a stepladder again!" the professor cried as Momo moved on to polishing the moose head mounted on the wall.

"Brilliant, Professor!" Beatrice exclaimed. "Although I did think the cobwebs looked rather nice."

Just then, Kneecap and Bonehead wandered into the living room. "What's going on?" Kneecap asked, rubbing her eye sockets.

"Cool!" Bonehead cried, catching sight of Momo. He ran toward the creature, who scooped the little skeleton up and put him on his shoulder.

"Fun ride fun fun!" Momo cried as he galloped around the room. Bonehead squealed with joy.

Wolf Man Stu groaned and opened his eyes, but when he saw Momo running around the living room with Bonehead on his back, he fainted again.

"Can I have a ride, too, Mom?" Kneecap asked.

"Um...maybe when you're older," Tibia said nervously.

The professor cupped his hands around his mouth. "It's time to put your new friend down, Momo!" he called.

Momo stopped in his tracks. Ever so gently, he plucked Bonehead from his back and set him on his feet.

"Thankth!" Bonehead said, holding up his hand. Momo gave him a high five, and the little skeleton staggered backward a few steps.

"Well, Professor, it seems we were wrong about you," Beatrice said. "This new creature of yours is useful and entertaining... and he almost makes up for the television you stole."

"Television?" the professor repeated.

Just then, Wolf Man Stu woke up again. He groaned and stood up. "Oh, my head," he said with a groan. "Does anyone have some aspirin?"

"I didn't take zee television," Professor Von Skalpel said. "Volf Man Schtu did!"

"You!" the Swamp Horror cried, turning to the werewolf. "I'll throw you in the swamp for this!"

Wolf Man Stu yelped and ran out of the living room, the Swamp Horror hot on his heels.

"Does this mean we don't get to ransack the lab?" Eye-Gore asked.

"Not this time," Beatrice said. "But who knows what tomorrow will bring! Professor," she added, turning to Von Skalpel, "perhaps you aren't as big a quack as I thought."

The professor beamed. That was the nicest thing Beatrice had ever said to him.

The Swamp Horror staggered back into the room, breathing hard.

"Did Stu get away?" Steve asked.

"Not exactly," the Horror replied with a grin. "He jumped in the swamp. He'll be cleaning slime out of his fur for weeks."

"Well, that's it, then," Count Snobula said. "Justice has been served, the professor is a genius, and the chandelier is clean. I'm going to bed."

"Me, too," Sally agreed. "I need my beauty sleep."

Momo rubbed two of his three eyes. "Momo sleepy," he said.

"Where will Momo sleep?" Kneecap asked

her mother. "Can he stay in the hallway with us?"

"Dude," Eye-Gore said, "that thing is bigger than half the rooms in this house!"

"Eye-Gore is right," Beatrice told the professor. "I'm afraid there's no good place for Momo at the Manor."

Professor Von Skalpel frowned. He had been so excited about his enormous creature that it had never occurred to him to wonder where he would put it.

"Momo could stay with me," the Swamp Horror suggested. "There's plenty of room out by the swamp."

"Momo like swamp!" the creature said eagerly.

The monsters agreed that this was the best solution, and soon everyone headed off to bed.

And no one slept more soundly than the victorious Professor Von Skalpel.

The next morning, the professor decided to take a stroll out to the radioactive swamp to check on his creature. There was no answer when Von Skalpel called his name, so he decided to check the swamp behind Horror's house.

"Momo?" the professor called. "Momo, Daddy is here!"

"Do you *mind*?" the Swamp Horror snapped as the professor walked to the edge of the swamp. "Can't you see I'm taking a bath?"

"Oh, sorry!" the professor said quickly. "I am just looking for Momo."

"Momo?" the Swamp Horror asked. "I couldn't find him when I got up this morning.

I thought he was with you."

Just then, a little red cap floated into view.

"Oh, no!" the Swamp Horror cried.

Clearly, Momo had gone for a swim in the early morning. And that was a very bad thing for Momo. The professor's creation was not made for swimming.

"I knew I should have made zat Monster Glue vaterproof!" the professor wailed. "Oh, zis is all my fault! Poor Momo did not know zat he vas not supposed to go into zee vater. Zee vater ruined my monster!"

"Don't be so hard on yourself, Professor," the Horror said. "It could have happened to anyone." The Swamp Horror considered this statement for a moment. "Well, it could have happened to anyone who likes to make creatures out of glued-together body parts," he added.

The Swamp Horror climbed out of the murky water. "Let's go to the Manor," he said, "and have some breakfast."

The professor smiled. "I vill bet Frankie has already made somesing good for us," Von

Skalpel said. Smiling, the professor realized that maybe his original creature—Frankie—wasn't so bad, after all. Sure, Frankie had scars...but he was sturdy. And he was a good friend. That was very important in a creation.

Even though Von Skalpel's latest experiment wasn't a success, the professor felt lucky. At least the Swamp Horror wasn't angry with him anymore. In fact, nobody was angry with him anymore. Wolf Man Stu had brought the TV back first thing in the morning, and the Femur kids had flopped in front of it to watch their favorite cartoons. Even Funnybone had shown up in the kitchen at breakfast time.

Now Von Skalpel was just a typical mad

scientist who lived peaceably with a bunch of monsters. Everything was back to normal.

Well—not exactly *normal*.

But you know what I mean.